Mariella Mystery

Investigates

The Spaghetti Yeti

Look out for more books about
Mariella Mystery

The Ghostly Guinea Pig
A Cupcake Conundrum
The Huge Hair Scare
The Curse of the Pampered Poodle

Mariella Mystery

Investigates

The Spaghetti Yeti

by
Kate
Pankhurst

Orion
Children's Books

First published in Great Britain in 2014

Orion Children's Books
a division of the Orion Publishing Group Ltd
Orion House
5 Upper St Martin's Lane
London WC2H 9EA
An Hachette UK company

1 3 5 7 9 10 8 6 4 2

A catalogue record for this book is available from the British Library.

ISBN 978 1 5101 0507 2

Printed and bound in Great Britain
by CPI Group (UK) Ltd, Croydon, CR0 4YY

www.orionbooks.co.uk

For Tom and Jenn x

mysterious
clam

me, in COOL sunglasses

Annoying
Alert

Pippa

Arthur

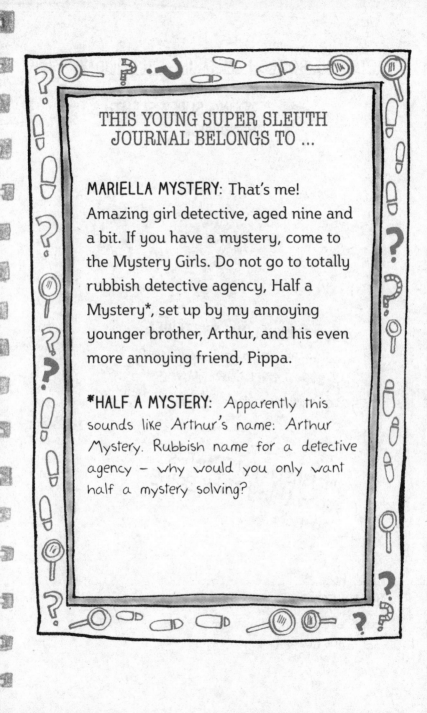

THIS YOUNG SUPER SLEUTH JOURNAL BELONGS TO ...

MARIELLA MYSTERY: That's me! Amazing girl detective, aged nine and a bit. If you have a mystery, come to the Mystery Girls. Do not go to totally rubbish detective agency, Half a Mystery*, set up by my annoying younger brother, Arthur, and his even more annoying friend, Pippa.

*HALF A MYSTERY: Apparently this sounds like Arthur's name: Arthur Mystery. Rubbish name for a detective agency — why would you only want half a mystery solving?

DETECTIVE BOOKS I AM TAKING ON HOLIDAY:

essential reading

YOUNG SUPER SLEUTH'S HANDBOOK

TOTALLY THRILLING MYSTERIES:

Amazing books about a team of detectives called The Fishy Four*, who solve mysteries in their school holidays.

"Fishsticks! There's something fishy going on here."

sally GUM

*FISHY FOUR: The gang got their name because Sally Gum has a cool detective catchphrase:

Monday 21st July

Woooooh! No more school — the holidays start here! The Mystery Girls' first ever team camping trip is TODAY!

FishyFour

kitty Seeker

woof

Sally Gum

McNally Gum

Pip

→ new mystery kit

8:00AM
IN THE BACK OF CAR, TRAVELLING
TO SALTY BAY (HOLIDAY DESTINATION)

I've been hoping that I'll have an amazing
adventure in my school holidays, like the ones
Sally Gum has in the Totally Thrilling Mystery
stories. But when I detected the first mystery of
the trip (before we'd even set off for Salty Bay)
it was NOT what I was expecting at all.

CASE REPORT: SALTY BAY CAMPING
TRIP: MYSTERY TEAM ASSEMBLED

6:00AM: The Mystery Girls are up
and ready to go. (Poppy and Violet slept
over.) We've given ourselves special roles so
we can be prepared for any mystery situation.

Poppy Holmes

Outdoor Outfit Organiser. Poppy says it's important to have a range of outfits for outdoor mystery solving. (I have told her not to get carried away with showy-off costumes like the ones she makes for her synchronised swimming team.)

Poppy →

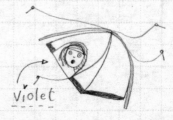

showy-off costumes

Violet Maple

Mystery Mayhem Monitor. Violet will be assessing the riskiness of mystery situations. (She has already made an escape plan in case the tent blows away with her in it.)

Violet →

Violet

Mariella Mystery

Mystery Magnet. I'll be looking for things to investigate. (Dark caves, secret passageways in abandoned lighthouses, that sort of thing.)

me ↓

SALTY BAY CAMPING TRIP: MYSTERIOUS EVENTS BEGIN

6:15AM: We should have set off by now but Mum and Dad forgot to set their alarm. Ugh, they KNOW the Mystery Girls have a

asleep ↓

lot of work to do at the campsite. Like setting up Mystery HQ and doing a sweep of the local area for a Totally Thrilling Mystery.

6:30AM: I overhear Dad having a whispered phone conversation. He says, "Don't worry, we haven't left yet. Drop her off as soon as you can." My Mystery Senses are tuned in. Who else is coming on our camping trip?

WHO IS THE MYSTERY CAMPER?

A: It can't be Granny Mystery — she vowed never to go camping again after the time she woke up with a slug on her nose.

slug

B: It's not Poppy and Violet. They are already here.

C: Mum and Dad have finally given in and got me a sniffer dog. This makes perfect sense because a camping holiday would be the ideal place to begin dog training.

slug

6:35AM: I tell Violet and Poppy the exciting news and decide to call the new puppy Shadow, because it's a really mysterious name.

Shadow

6:45AM: The doorbell rings and I race to answer it. Dad shouts, "Wait! There's something we haven't told you." I tell Dad that you can't surprise a trained detective. I already know about Shadow.

6:47AM: I open the door. There is no puppy. Only a Peanut.

The Peanut

Pippa Patterson, Arthur's stupid friend. (Me, Poppy and Violet have called her the Peanut ever since Arthur pushed a peanut up her nose and she had to go to hospital to have it removed.)

The PEANUT ↙

6:48AM: I conclude that a whole week of being around Pippa and Arthur will most probably be like having a peanut stuck up your nose. TOTALLY ANNOYING.

CASE CLOSED.

no!

our car

9:15AM
STILL IN CAR, 85 MILES FROM MY HOUSE

I am so annoyed. Mum and Dad only agreed
to let Poppy and Violet come after eight days
of intensive nagging about how a week apart
could ruin our chances of turning professional.
(This is a technique from the Young Super
Sleuth's Handbook called 'applying pressure to
witnesses'.) And now I find they've invited the
Peanut along, just like that.

The Peanut

I'm sure Mum only agreed because she has been stressed about Sheep Fest and the Knit-Your-Own-Swimming-Costume workshop she is running there on Saturday. (Mum owns an online knitting shop, Knitted Fancies – You Name it, We'll Knit It.)

knitted swimming costume

She said being invited to the festival was a big honour in the knitting world and that it was the perfect opportunity to visit Salty Bay, which is really nearby.

Hopefully we'll be too busy to even notice Arthur and the Peanut. I'm sure we'll uncover something mysterious really quickly. Salty Bay might seem like a sleepy seaside town, but in Totally Thrilling Mysteries that's *exactly* the sort of place where detectives uncover the best mysteries.

POOR QUALITY

In *A Smuggler's Sandwich*, the Fishy Four expose a smuggling ring* that is using a quiet fishing port to smuggle poor-quality sandwich fillings into the country.

*SMUGGLING RING: This is when a group of people (smugglers) try to sneak something into the country that isn't allowed. Like stolen jewellery or pet tortoises.

illegal tortoise

smuggler

This could be the most exciting week of our mystery-solving lives. A whole six days together with no school – in a tent. Wow!

Us having an adventure!

SUMMER HOLIDAY MYSTERIES:

Day-to-day cases involving missing pets, lost property and petty vandalism need a professional eye but can, after a while, become boring to investigate. School holidays are an excellent opportunity to uncover mysteries full of adventure and intrigue.

Packing Essentials:

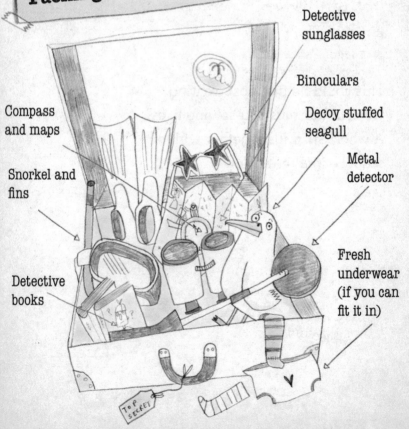

Detective sunglasses

Binoculars

Decoy stuffed seagull

Metal detector

Compass and maps

Snorkel and fins

Fresh underwear (if you can fit it in)

Detective books

Spotting the Signs

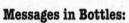

Spooky Shipwrecks:
Often found in deserted
coves. Can be a centre
for paranormal activity.

Messages in Bottles:
If anyone has been
kidnapped in the local area
they may send a message
for help this way.

Abandoned Fairgrounds:
The perfect setting for criminal
activity. Watch out for sinister
fortune tellers.

**Ancient Treasure
Maps:** Often hidden
under the floorboards
of old holiday cottages.

WARNING

Wear a sun hat on surveillance
missions to avoid sunburn.
Nobody will take a bright red
detective seriously.

More lobster
than detective

Cool as a
cucumber

1:45PM
LIMPET ROCKS CAMPSITE, ON OUR
CAMPING PITCH

After what felt like the longest car journey ever, we caught our first glimpse of the town of Salty Bay. A collection of old buildings jumbled in a cove, surrounded by steep cliffs and sparkling sea. At last! We were finally about to arrive at what was hopefully a hotspot for mystery and adventure!

Salty Bay

When we parked outside the campsite reception, a smiling man and woman wearing Limpet Rocks ROCKS! t-shirts were waiting.

Jake and Jemima

"Welcome!" said the lady. "I'm Jemima, and this is Jake. We run Limpet Rocks Campsite. It rocks!"

They gave us a guided tour before showing us to our pitch. This place is brilliant! It overlooks Salty Bay and is jam-packed with colourful tents and caravans. There are people lounging in deckchairs and groups of kids laughing and throwing beach balls.

There's also a collection of log cabin shops and restaurants, and one of them is an ice-cream parlour called Chill Your Beans! AMAZING. There's a café called the Limpet Lounger and a cool souvenir shop called the Sparkling Starfish.

"Wow! This campsite has everything – we won't ever have to leave," Mum said.

Mum is right, and if we weren't on the hunt for a mystery, I'd totally stay here all week. It's so cool. Our tent location is perfect. We're right on the edge of the camping field, with the woods behind. (Could be useful for hiding in if we need to avoid angry smugglers.)

Arthur and the Peanut tried to pitch their tent next to ours, but I said no way, so now they are opposite (still too close for my liking). Mum and Dad are next door, though I've tried to make sure we are far enough away not to be overheard when we have top-secret mystery meetings.

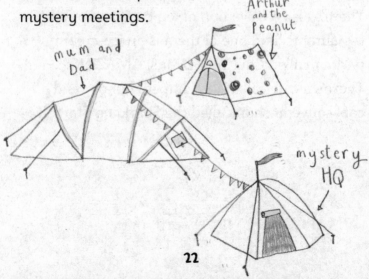

Arthur and the Peanut

mum and Dad

mystery HQ

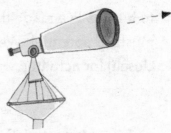

3:20PM
LIMPET ROCKS CAMPSITE, CLIFF TOP
VIEWING POINT

Our first sweep of the campsite for mysterious
avenues* to explore is complete. So much for
Half a Mystery – Arthur and the Peanut have run
off with some kids from a few tents away to join
the Wheeny Whelks Rock Pool Raiders group.

*MYSTERIOUS AVENUE: This is when you pick a
line of enquiry or something that needs looking
into. Also sounds like it would be the perfect
street for a detective to live on.

I can confirm that current mystery levels appear to be low. I've made this map of areas with mystery potential. We will be monitoring them closely for activity:

yum

3:45PM
CHILL YOUR BEANS! ICE-CREAM PARLOUR, LIMPET ROCKS CAMPSITE

Poppy wanted to visit the on-site ice-cream parlour. She says it's important to keep our Mystery Senses refreshed, especially if we want to uncover a mystery.

The ice-cream parlour is definitely a great place to 'chill your beans' and relax. The speakers are playing sounds of the sea and it's full of campers sitting on squishy beanbags, eating enormous sundaes.

There didn't seem to be anyone serving, so we checked out the different flavours at the counter.

"Is that...baked bean flavour?" said Violet, pointing to a pale orange ice-cream. I deduced that anyone who thinks baked bean ice-cream might be nice must be completely bonkers.

And I was right, because just then Jake burst through the door behind the counter dressed as a starfish, followed by Jemima, who was wearing a huge red crab costume.

starfish

"CHILL YOUR BEANS!" Jake shouted. He seemed really out of breath.

"Would you girls like to try the baked bean ice-cream?" said Jemima.

CRAB

Jake and Jemima were so nice, it felt mean to say no. But the baked bean ice-cream really did look disgusting.

"COOL costumes," Poppy said.
(Good distraction tactic, Poppy.)

"Thanks! We always wear them for the Wheeny Whelks Rock Pool Raiders Session," said Jemima.

"Do you run this place as well as the Wheeny Whelks activities then?" I asked.

"Yes, and the souvenir shop and café. We want this campsite to have everything for the perfect holiday," Jake said, grinning.

Wow. When Jake and Jemima said they ran Limpet Rocks, I didn't realise they were the only ones working here.

"If you like our costumes, you might enjoy the costume parade on Friday night," said Jemima. "There's a prize for the best one."

"Amazing! Count us in," Poppy said. She had that expression on her face she gets whenever she hears about competitions. (She loves them.)

Costume *Parade* BUFFET PRIZES FUN PARTY! Friday 7:30pm Pow-Wow Area

When we've finished our ice-creams (luckily not baked bean flavour), we are going to keep looking for a mystery. Poppy is already going on about how the costume parade could be an excellent opportunity to showcase disguises for future investigations. I hope she isn't going to get distracted from what we are here to do.

poppy's ideas

THE SHELL

DETECTIVE OCTOPUS

DETECTIVE OF THE FUTURE

marsh mallow

crackle!

7:30PM
MYSTERY GIRLS HQ, TOASTING MARSHMALLOWS

I know I shouldn't expect mysterious stuff to happen straightaway, but so far Salty Bay does seem to be just a quiet seaside town. Limpet Rocks is so amazing, I was expecting Salty Bay to be the same. It couldn't be more different.

As we walked down the path to the town we spotted another ice-cream parlour opposite the campsite. It's called Bella's. I was really excited about having TWO ice-cream parlours we could use for mystery meetings, but up close, it was dark and empty.

Bella's ice-cream

Bit rubbish

29

On the High Street, there was hardly anyone
about. The shops are all really old and the
shopkeepers seem totally bored, as if nothing
exciting has happened for years. We saw another
holiday park too – Bay Bottom. Full of rusty old
caravans. I'm glad we aren't staying there.

It's lucky Limpet Rocks is so brilliant, because
the only mysterious thing to have happened
all day was when Half a Mystery launched an
investigation into an abandoned swimming cap.
(Not even slightly mysterious.)

"Maybe we'll spot suspicious activity tonight, like secret torch signals in the bay," I said.

"Maybe," said Violet. "And if not, look on the bright side – if we had a mystery to solve, we might miss out on all the fun. There's a Learn-to-Swim-Like-a-Mermaid class tomorrow!"

"But what if nothing mysterious happens the whole holiday?" I said. (Violet is very relaxed about our current non-mystery situation. I'm not.)

"Well, we could practise some new mystery-solving techniques, like designing amazing disguises for the parade," Poppy said.

Hmmmm. They do have a point. The Young Super Sleuth's Handbook says that keeping your skills up to date is important. And toasting marshmallows on the campfire is fun. But it isn't what I've been getting excited about for weeks.

yum

Mallow Mellows

martha

9:05PM
OUTSIDE TENT OF MARTHA MAYHEW
(THREE TENTS AWAY FROM US)

The Young Super Sleuth's Handbook says to
be prepared for anything at any time. But I
could NEVER have been prepared for what's
just happened!

After dinner, Mum said we
should all do an activity together.
She suggested sorting out wool
for Sheep Fest (boring), but I said
ghost stories around the campfire
would be much better. It's just the
sort of thing the Fishy Four do when
they are having rare quiet moments.

WOOL
(BORING)

To turn up the creepiness to maximum levels I got Violet to hold a torch under my chin, which makes your face look totally scary and shadowy, like something out of a horror film.

sinister!

I started reading from Totally Thrilling Mysteries, *Ghost of a Goldfish*. The story is set in a rundown holiday cottage. Sally Gum takes her pet goldfish along, but problems start when he mysteriously vanishes.

Sally tried not to think about how much she missed Sparkle. She concentrated on the sound of the old grandfather clock instead.

tick tock

Tick tock. Tick tock. SPLASH! Splash! Splash!

What was that? Sally edged closer to the bathroom, where the frantic sloshing sound was coming from.

Was it the tap dripping?
No, that was turned off.
SPLASH!

Sally shifted her glance to
the toilet. Then she saw him.

"ARRR**GGGG**ggggg**GHHH**hhh!"

Honestly, I thought, Arthur and the Peanut are
such wimps! The ghost of the goldfish in the toilet
isn't even the scariest bit. That's when I realised
the screams weren't coming from them, or
anyone else round our campfire.

"ARrrgrggghhhh**HHHHH!**"

It was from the woods behind our tent. And if I've
learned one thing in my time as a detective, it's
that a scream from dark woods usually means
something mysterious is going on.

EYEWITNESS REPORT: MARTHA MAYHEW

8:45PM: Martha is preparing spaghetti bolognese over the campfire. She is ready to serve dinner, but needs a cheese grater. Martha sends her husband, Dave, into the tent to get it.

spaghetti bolognese

8:47PM: Dave shouts that he can't see the cheese grater. This is typical – Dave is rubbish at finding stuff. Martha goes to get the grater herself.

8:51PM: When Martha comes back outside the pan of spaghetti is no longer over the campfire. Weird. Martha looks around at the other campers nearby. Has one of them pinched her dinner?

8:53PM: CRACK! Martha hears a twig snapping in the woods behind her tent. Is it the spaghetti thief? She goes to investigate.

WOODS

8:56PM: Martha freezes. A large bush approximately five metres ahead of her is moving.

8:57PM: The bush is not a bush. It is some sort of creature. Martha isn't sure what it is, but as it stands to its full height, she knows it's not human. It's too big. Too hairy. Too terrifying. It's holding the spaghetti pan, and has its horrible glowing yellow eyes fixed on her. Martha turns and runs screaming from the woods.

NEW MYSTERY TO SOLVE: WHAT TOTALLY WEIRD, SPAGHETTI-STEALING CREATURE IS LURKING IN THE WOODS?

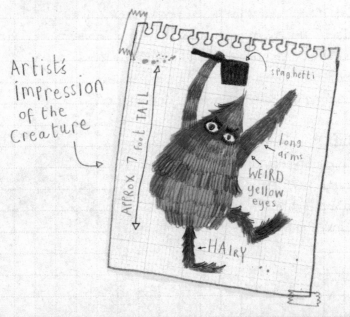

Artist's impression of the creature

spaghetti

APPROX 7 foot TALL

long arms

WEIRD yellow eyes

← HAIRY

9:30PM
MYSTERY GIRLS HQ, EMERGENCY MYSTERY GIRL MEETING (YAY!)

Mum said not to get all worked up because there is probably a logical explanation, but this is too weird to ignore. Weirder still is the theory Poppy has come up with.

In the car on the way here, Poppy was reading a book about mysterious animals and she has realised that what Martha described seems remarkably like a creature well known in mysterious circles*:

*MYSTERIOUS CIRCLES: Groups of mystery solvers. Me, Poppy and Violet move in mysterious circles together.

THE YETI (AKA BIGFOOT)

Rumoured to look like a large bear or ape. Has been reported as being aggressive towards humans.

Distinguishing Features: Hairy, seven foot tall, large feet, long arms.

Thought to live in remote mountainous areas like the Himalayas.

A blurry photo

Footprint

The Himalayas in Nepal

A potential yeti-in-the-woods mystery is just the sort of thing we've been hoping for! We're trying not to get carried away, though – not without more evidence.

"It does seem unlikely," I said. "Nobody knows if yetis exist and other reported sightings have been miles away. I'm pretty sure the Himalayas are nowhere near Salty Bay."

"There can't possibly be a yeti living in the campsite woods. Where would it have come from?" said Violet.

"What if the yeti has always been here? What if there's a local legend – you know, like the Loch Ness Monster?" said Poppy.

"Yeah, right," said Violet. "The Legendary Spaghetti Yeti of Salty Bay."

None of us is sure what Martha saw so we have run through all the logical explanations:

LOGICAL EXPLANATION ONE:

It has been very hot today and Martha is suffering from sunstroke. Sunstroke can cause hallucinations, such as seeing a yeti-like creature in the woods.
(Doesn't explain what happened to the spaghetti.)

sun tan cream

sunburn

LOGICAL (Possible) EXPLANATION TWO:

A creature did steal Martha's spaghetti, but it was a big fox or badger or somebody's pet cat. It was hungry and attracted to the campsite by the smell of Martha's dinner. (Can foxes, badgers or cats carry pans of spaghetti — or grow scarily big?)

Fox

Badger

LOGICAL (NOT VERY LIKELY) EXPLANATION THREE:

Martha did see a yeti. But why would one be in Salty Bay? Do yetis even eat spaghetti? Is there a local legend we don't know about?

nom nom!

VERDICT: Tomorrow we will speak to campsite owners, Jake and Jemima. (Mum says we have to go to bed now.) They could have had similar reports in the past and be able to explain what this thing is.

Tuesday 22nd July

RARR!

Scary woodland creatures?

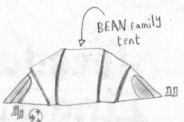
BEAN family tent

9:00AM
OUTSIDE TENT OF THE BEAN FAMILY (FIVE TENTS AWAY FROM MYSTERY HQ)

When we woke up this morning, Martha's story about a scary spaghetti-stealing creature seemed even more unbelievable than it did last night.

Other campers were eating breakfast by their tents, and Arthur and the Peanut were helping Dad fry bacon on the camping stove. Only Martha looked upset. On the way to the shower block we saw her sitting on a deckchair staring into space. When her husband knocked over a stack of pans, she jumped up in shock.

Yeti or not, whatever Martha saw spooked her – that's why we need to investigate.

spooked

We were heading to find Jake and Jemima, when we passed a woman standing outside her tent. She was shaking her head at a pile of food scattered on the ground. I knew we couldn't ignore any unusual incidents involving food.

"Is everything OK?" I asked.

"I said camping was a terrible idea – creepy-crawlies, wild animals. And now THIS!" the woman said.

I looked closely at the mushed-up boxes of Choco Pops, burger buns and tins. It all seemed to be covered in some kind of orange goo. Poppy dipped her finger in.

alphabetti spaghetti!

"It's spaghetti sauce," she said, amazed. "Alphabetti Spaghetti, to be precise."

Violet gasped. I can't believe that just last night we thought this place was totally unmysterious!

EYEWITNESS REPORT: EMMA BEAN

3:00AM: Emma Bean is woken by loud snoring. She is wearing earplugs, so at first it is just mildly annoying.

3:10AM: The snoring is still going on. Emma pulls out her earplugs. She realises the noise isn't coming from any of her sleeping family — it's outside and it's more like heavy, raspy breathing than snoring.

earplugs

3:11AM: Emma shakes her husband, Barry. She tells him there is a wild animal outside. He says this is all part of the camping experience and she should go back to sleep.

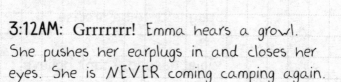

3:12AM: Grrrrrrr! Emma hears a growl. She pushes her earplugs in and closes her eyes. She is *NEVER* coming camping again.

8:10AM: After very little sleep Emma goes outside and discovers the food for the whole holiday scattered around the tent.
She decides to complain to the campsite owners. They clearly need an electric fence to keep all forms of wildlife out.

NOTE: Most of the food hasn't been eaten, just trampled and messed up. From a four pack of Alphabetti Spaghetti, three tins are missing — the one left has been pierced, spraying spaghetti and sauce everywhere.

VERDICT: We only have one confirmed sighting, but that's twice now spaghetti has been targeted, so we are assuming that both incidents were carried out by the same creature. What kind of badger, fox or squirrel can break open a tin can? Was this the work of a larger, scarier spaghetti-loving yeti?

45

10:00AM
LIMPET LOUNGER CAFÉ

We found Jake and Jemima outside the campsite
shops and cafés. They had already spoken to
Martha and Emma.

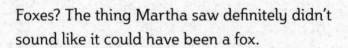
cheeky fox?

"Foxes can be very
cheeky. We've had
problems with them
stealing food before,"
said Jemima, shaking
her head.

Foxes? The thing Martha saw definitely didn't
sound like it could have been a fox.

"Have you ever seen a fox as big as the one
Martha described?" I asked.

"Well, no. And we've never had reports of pans of spaghetti going missing or foxes with glowing yellow eyes," said Jake. "I'm sure it's nothing to worry about – but we'll issue advice on storing food so it doesn't attract wildlife."

"What if it was something else?" Poppy said. "Like a yeti."

Jemima smiled. "Well, we've been here for six months and not yet met a yeti." She winked, then she and Jake went off to open the shops.

"Well, that was easy, wasn't it? No yeti, just a hungry fox," said Violet.

But Jake and Jemima just said they'd never heard of a fox like the one Martha saw, so how can we be sure the spaghetti stealer was one?

Peanut

11:00AM
SALTY BAY TOWN CENTRE, OUTSIDE SMOKE AND MIRRORS (FANCY-DRESS SHOP)

We have decided to come into town to talk to the local shop owners and find out if they know of any legends about a weird creature. Jake and Jemima have only been at the campsite for six months so there must be loads of things they don't know about the area.

Annoyingly, Mum has made us bring Arthur and the Peanut so she can practise her Sheep Fest knitting workshop on Dad. How are we supposed to investigate properly with those two hanging around?

NO!

The cobbled High Street was empty again when we arrived. Even though the shops sell similar stuff to the campsite, it all looks so dusty and old, I can see why nobody bothers to come here.

There was one place that we didn't spot yesterday – an amazing fancy-dress shop with a fairy tale characters display in the window. There was a Little Red Riding Hood, a wolf, Cinderella and a troll with massive hairy feet.

dusty old stuff!

Smoke and Mirrors

troll

Poppy was really excited. "This is exactly how I want the Mystery Girls' Disguise Storeroom to look one day!" she said, running inside. "WOW. Check this out!" Her eyes were fixed on a wig made from strands of silver glitter.

glitter wig

SCARY BROWS

A door behind the counter swung open and a woman wearing a sequinned crop top and leggings stepped out. Her hair was pulled back in a bun so tight it looked as if her eyebrows might pop off her face.

"Can't you read?!" she snapped. "The sign in the window says one child at a time."

"Actually, we are the Mystery Girls and we wanted to ..." I began.

"This isn't just an ordinary fancy-dress shop, you know. It's a theatrical supplies shop – Olga De Bouffet's Smoke and Mirrors*," the woman said. (I have deduced this must be Olga De Bouffet.)

*SMOKE AND MIRRORS: Tricking or deceiving somebody, like you could with lots of smoke and mirrors, or fancy-dress costumes.

"Professional actors, like myself, come here for their stage costumes. I can't have the shop crowded with children. It's been the same ever since that awful campsite started its weekly costume parade."

Olga gestured towards a series of framed photographs of a woman on stage. They were all of a much younger Olga (I have also deduced that Olga De Bouffet is a bit of a show-off.)

slightly less scary

"How much is the glitter wig?" Poppy asked.

"It's not for sale," said Olga, glaring. "It's the only one left and I need it for display. Now, off you go. Like I said, one child at a time."

"Well, if we can't have the glitter wig, we'll ALL be leaving," Poppy said, pulling me and Violet out of the shop. Arthur and the Peanut ran after us.

"So rude," said Poppy. "We could have totally used a glitter wig to win the costume parade – I can't believe she wouldn't sell it to us."

We're hoping other shopkeepers will be more helpful.

HORRIBLE

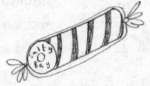

11:45AM
OUTSIDE ROCKY ROADS' ROCK SHOP

Rocky Roads' Rock Shop was empty except for the shopkeeper, Mr Roads, who was talking to a man wearing a Bay Bottom Holiday Park T-shirt, with a badge which read, 'Manager'.

"Customers!" Mr Roads said, like he was totally surprised to have some. "What can I do for you? How about a rock cooked breakfast?"

MR Roads

rock cooked breakfast

ROCK
unicorn
↓

"We're the Mystery Girls," I said. "We're staying at Limpet Rocks and we wondered if we could ask you about the local area?"

The manager of Bay Bottom glared at us, then tutted and walked out of the shop, slamming the door behind him. (What is wrong with people in this town?)

"Don't mind him. There aren't many fans of your campsite in Salty Bay," Mr Roads said. "Not since it changed to an everything-you-could-ever-need-under-one-roof fancy-pants place. Those two are sending us all out of business."

Glare

BAY BOTTOM

Mr Roads looked sadly around his empty shop.

"What did you want to know?" he said.
And are you sure I can't interest
you in an everlasting stick
of rock?" He pointed
to some sticks of
rock in faded
wrappers.

I was about to politely say "No, thanks" when the
Peanut piped up in her squeaky peanut voice.

"What's your favourite colour?"

Argh! I knew she and Arthur would be totally
annoying if we brought them. I decided to get
straight to the point, as professionally as I could.

"We wanted to know if you'd ever heard any
local legends about a large creature living in
the woods," I said.

"Yeah, a lady on our campsite saw a hairy yeti with yellow eyes. It likes bolognese and alphabetti spaghetti. And I'm not even a little bit scared," Arthur said. "Mum says I'm a big boy now." Honestly, what sort of detective says their mum thinks they are a big boy?

"That's partly right," I said, pushing him out of the way. "We are investigating a strange sighting of a creature spotted by somebody staying on our campsite."

Mr Roads was quiet for a moment. He looked thoughtful and I hoped he might be about to tell us about an ancient spooky legend. But then he said, "You're in the wrong town for monsters. Nothing like that here. Can I interest you in some Loch Ness Monster-shaped rock? Or some rock spaghetti?"

spaghetti rock →

nessie rock

5:35PM
OUTSIDE CAMPSITE GATES

NEW DEVELOPMENT ALERT!

We were feeling fed up when we got back
from the town. After Mr Roads, the shop
owners at Salty Bay Supplies, Salty Fudge
Shop and Coconut Shack Beachwear all looked
at us blankly when we asked about local
legends, then tried to sell us stuff.
Arthur and the Peanut actually
bought a completely
embarrassing hat.

Fake
seagull

weird
FROG souvenir
made of shells

Every single one of the shopkeepers complained about how their shops had always been busy until Jake and Jemima came along. Some of them were quite horrible about the campsite.

It was a relief to get back to the happy holiday atmosphere of Limpet Rocks – even if the afternoon had been a total waste of time.

TUM tum **TE TUM, TUM TUM TE TUMMMM** Te **TUM TUM.**

An ice cream van drove out from the car park of the deserted ice-cream parlour across the road.

It pulled up next to us, and a woman with a swirled-up hairstyle stuck her head out of the serving hatch.

swirled up

"I saw you walking back from town. Bit quiet, was it?" she asked.

The last thing I felt like was another conversation about Limpet Rocks stealing everyone's customers – we'd had enough of that in town. Luckily, the ice-cream lady just shook her head and smiled.

"Sorry – no point dwelling on it. If the customers don't come to you, go to them, that's what I always say! Easy when you have an ice-cream van. Bella Gelato's the name," she smiled. "Now, how about an ice-cream? The first one is on the house. Once you try it, you'll never visit Chill Your Beans! again."

Free ice-cream – this was more like it! I deduced
Bella must be the owner of Bella's Ice-Cream
Parlour and that she was the friendliest Salty Bay
local we had met so far.

"The Gelato family has been
making ice-cream in Salty Bay
for many years," she said,
handing us our cones.

Free
ice-cream

Brilliant, I thought. Bella is sure to know about all
the local legends.

"Bella, you are just the person we need to speak
to," I said seriously. "Have you ever heard about
a weird creature who likes spaghetti living in
the woods?"

And all of a sudden Bella wasn't a smiley ice-
cream lady any more. Her face fell and she
looked really worried. That's when, before
she even told us, I knew Bella must have seen
something too.

EYEWITNESS REPORT: BELLA GELATO
STRANGE EVENTS ON MONDAY EVENING

11:55PM: Passing Limpet Rocks Campsite on her way home for the day, Bella thinks what a pleasant evening it is. Out of nowhere, a huge shadowy figure darts over the campsite wall into the road ahead. Bella slams on the brakes.

11:56PM: The van narrowly misses the figure and comes to a halt on a grass verge. Bella tells herself it must have been a camper, somebody who got lost on the way to the toilets. But deep down she knows that isn't what she saw.

11:57PM: Bella looks in her wing mirror. There's nothing there. Just an empty road. Did she imagine it?

worried

11:58PM: RAAAARRRRRRR!
A terrifying hairy figure with yellow glowing eyes leaps up at Bella's side window.

11:59PM: The van's tyres squeal as Bella pushes the accelerator to the floor and drives away as fast as she can.

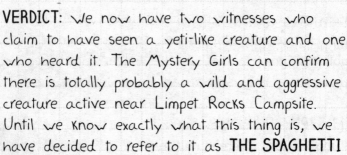

NOTE: This is an artist's impression of what Bella saw. Her description matches the one Martha provided.

VERDICT: We now have two witnesses who claim to have seen a yeti-like creature and one who heard it. The Mystery Girls can confirm there is totally probably a wild and aggressive creature active near Limpet Rocks Campsite. Until we know exactly what this thing is, we have decided to refer to it as **THE SPAGHETTI YETI**. This sounds catchier than Great-Big-Hairy-Thing-In-The-Woods-That-Looks-Like-A-Yeti. (It also accurately describes the creature's appearance and known eating habits.)

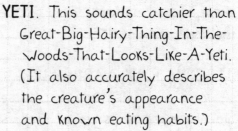

SPAGHETTI YETI

6:30PM
MYSTERY HQ, WEIRD CREATURE ANALYSIS COMPLETE

My head is spinning. Our research has revealed no local legends about yetis in Salty Bay, and we're sure ordinary woodland animals like squirrels or foxes can't mutate into yetis. We have even checked the local papers to see if any massive animals, like gorillas, have escaped from nearby zoos, but there is nothing.

MUTANT squirrel

So how do we explain what our witnesses saw?

This is what we have come up with:

POSSIBLE REASONS FOR A YETI IN SALTY BAY

1. The yeti got lost trying to find the Himalayas and accidentally wandered into Salty Bay.

frozen

2. The yeti has been preserved in a block of ice in the woods since prehistoric times. The ice recently melted in the hot weather and set the yeti free.

3. The yeti has been hibernating in the woods for millions of years and was woken by the cooking smells from the new campsite which sent it crazy for spaghetti-based foods.

VERDICT: All of these seem very unlikely. This is totally one of the weirdest cases we've ever investigated. If we are going to figure out what this thing is, we need to see it for ourselves.

11:07PM
DOORWAY OF MYSTERY GIRLS HQ, ALL-NIGHT SURVEILLANCE MISSION

Campsite status: Mostly quiet apart from the sound of campers getting ready for bed. Sky is clear. Good conditions for Spaghetti Yeti spotting. We are staying up all night to keep watch.

I told Mum we wanted to search the woods but she says we aren't allowed to wander around in the dark when there have been reports of a weird creature – or ever. Which is rubbish, because so far, the creature has only been active at night. We have decided to keep watch from here and hope the creature walks past our tent looking for more spaghetti.

yeti

"I don't like this," said Violet. (She is insisting we have a torch on at all times.) "What if the creature sees us?"

"We could trap it, so it can go back to wherever it came from!" Poppy said.

TRAPPED

DANGER yeti

"Poppy is right," I said. "But it's no good just finding out what this thing is – we need to stop it causing any more trouble."

"HOW are we going to do that?" Violet said.

I have no idea. It's a good thing we've got all night to think about it. Wait, what's that? It's some sort of shuffling at the back of the tent.

SPAGHETTI YETI ALERT!

11:20PM
STILL IN MYSTERY HQ, ON ALL-NIGHT SURVEILLANCE

False alarm. It was Arthur and the Peanut.

"We heard you talking about wanting to go into the woods at night," said the Peanut. "And we've come up with a plan."

Arthur held up a poster:

Come and Join the
WILDLIFE WANDER
WEDNESDAY NIGHT 8PM
SEE SOME FANTASTIC
NOCTURNAL WILDLIFE!

"We've asked Mum and she says we can go because it's an organised trip!" said Arthur.

I was about to go crazy at them for listening to private Mystery Girl meetings when Poppy interrupted.

"Erm, that's actually a really good idea," she said.

Now that I've thought about it, it is quite good. The Wildlife Wander is the perfect opportunity to track and trap the yeti at night without getting into trouble with Mum and Dad. (I'm pretty sure this was just a one-off good idea from Half a Mystery and we don't need to worry about them suddenly becoming better detectives than us.)

Still RUbbish

Wednesday
23rd July

weird
alert

7:45AM
MYSTERY HQ

I've just woken up in the doorway of the tent with my plan for how to catch the creature stuck to my cheek. Poppy was lying face down on her costume sketches for the parade and Violet was snoring her head off. (How did that not wake me up sooner?)

I can't believe it – the Spaghetti Yeti could have been doing anything while I've been asleep!

SNORING!

I shook them both awake. "We were meant to be on all-night surveillance! Get up," I said.

"I think we did quite well, considering it was our first attempt," Violet said sleepily.

Violet seems to be missing the point of all-night surveillance, which is that you are meant to stay awake all night. At least I managed to come up with a way of restraining the creature before I dozed off. We'll need some specialist equipment, but it shouldn't be too hard to get hold of:

HOW TO CATCH YETI.

RARR!

yeti

Large net

Trapped

Now Violet is trying to find her toothbrush and Poppy says she needs to redo her sketches for the costumes because she dribbled on them in her sleep. You'd think there wasn't an urgent mystery situation going on at all!

starfish

9:00AM
OUTSIDE THE SPARKLING STARFISH,
CAMPSITE SOUVENIR SHOP

I wanted to check the campsite for signs of
yeti activity straightaway and get supplies for
yeti trapping, but Mum and Dad made us eat
breakfast first. (As if we have time for trivial
things like breakfast!) When we finally started
our search of the campsite, we spotted something
near the shops.

Jake and Jemima were talking to three campers
who were still wearing their pyjamas. I deduced
that if the campers hadn't got dressed yet, they
must have needed to speak to Jake and Jemima
urgently. It didn't take a genius to work out what
it was about.

YETI ACTIVITY LAST NIGHT:

ROSE AND TED POSSET (TENT LOCATED IN CENTRE OF CAMPSITE)

1:00AM: Rose and Ted wake to the sound of growling outside their tent. They go to investigate and discover their food has been thrown around and a tin of ravioli is missing.

PATRICIA PARKINSON (PITCHED NEAR OUR TENT WITH HER FRIEND, MELISSA)

2:10AM: Patricia is at the toilet block cleaning her teeth when she hears a terrifying growl. Patricia had spaghetti on toast for dinner last night — did the smell of it attract the creature?

MICHAEL HARDBOTTOM (STAYING IN THE BIGGEST TENT ON THE CAMPSITE WITH HIS FAMILY)

3:20AM: Michael gets up to investigate a banging noise. He discovers the tent door open and food scattered everywhere. A pack of dried spaghetti is missing.

EVIDENCE (NOT VERY CONCLUSIVE):

HAIRBRUSH: Belongs to Melissa. Located in toilet block.

STRANDS OF GLITTER:

Found mixed in with messed-up food. Poppy thinks this is from one of those wigs she wanted from Olga's shop. Did the creature rip it apart, thinking it was strands of spaghetti?

NOTE: Poppy has lost focus. She is worried other campers have glitter wigs and that we now don't stand a chance in the costume parade. We have bigger things to worry about.

LOST FOCUS

VERDICT: The Spaghetti Yeti has been driven wild by the taste of spaghetti and its attacks are getting more daring. On tonight's Wildlife Wander we need to trap it before the situation gets worse.

12:30PM
OUTSIDE THE LIMPET LOUNGER CAFÉ

The holiday atmosphere from yesterday feels as though it's had a bucket of chilly seawater chucked all over it. Everyone is talking about the Spaghetti Yeti.

The scariness was too much for Martha. (That's what she told Mum.) When she heard the creature had been back, she and her husband booked in at the Bay Bottom Holiday Park. (That rusty caravan place we saw in the town yesterday.)

Martha and Dave

Quite a few other campers thought this was a good idea too and have started packing up. Jemima has been trying her best to persuade them to stay, but she can't answer any of their questions about what the creature actually is or how it can be stopped. Jake looks flustered and worried. I feel really sorry for them. None of this is their fault.

Jemima

Jake

"I should let everyone know that the Wildlife Wander tonight is off," we heard Jake say to Jemima.

This was bad. The Wildlife Wander could be our only chance to catch the yeti.

"NO!" I said, running over. "You still need to make sure everyone has a fantastic holiday doing exciting stuff! We're still here, and we were really looking forward to it."

Jemima thought for a moment. "Mariella is right, Jake. If we start cancelling activities, even more people will leave," she said.

Phew. But we didn't get to feel relieved for long, because a short woman wearing a grey suit was marching across the campsite towards us.

"Are you the people in charge of this place?" the woman snapped at Jake and Jemima. "Numpton, that's my name. Agatha Numpton. Salty Bay Safety Officer."

Agatha numpton

77

"I've heard some disturbing reports that this campsite has a wild animal problem," she continued. "What's being done about this? I've closed establishments down for less. Salty Seafront Snacks didn't last five minutes after they refused to tackle those seagull attacks."

"Closed down?" Jemima gasped.

"Surely there's no need for that!" Jake said.

"I think we'll start with a full campsite safety inspection," Agatha said, ignoring them both.

Jake and Jemima had no choice but to dash after Agatha as she strode off across the campsite, marking things on her clipboard.

I knew this was a serious mystery situation, but the campsite actually being shut down? That's so unfair! We need to figure out our plan – and quickly.

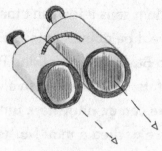

3:30PM
MYSTERY GIRL HQ, PREPARING TO TRACK
AND TRAP A YETI

After the inspection, Jake told
us that Agatha gave them an
Official Warning. Apparently
she said that the moment she
hears another wild animal
report she won't hesitate to take
stronger action, like closing the
campsite. This means we can't
afford any mistakes on the
Wildlife Wander. We have to catch
this thing.

OFFICIAL
WARNING
FOR BEING
UNSAFE
DUE TO WILD
ANIMAL PROBLEM

Mum says if it wasn't for Sheep Fest on Saturday, we'd be going home too. Dad looked into moving to Bay Bottom Holiday Park, but with so many of us, it's too expensive. I'm glad. There's no way we can go anywhere until we've solved this case. I've packed a mini-Mystery Kit with all the essentials we'll need for tonight.

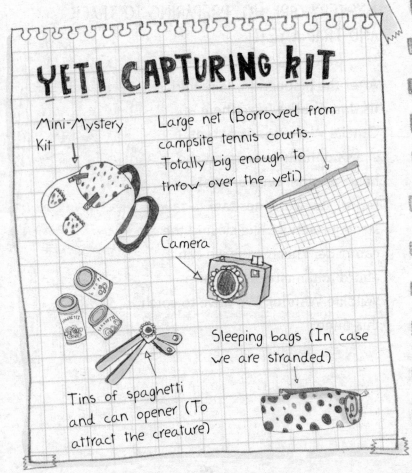

YETI CAPTURING KiT

Mini-Mystery Kit ↓

Large net (Borrowed from campsite tennis courts. Totally big enough to throw over the yeti) ↘

Camera ↘

Tins of spaghetti and can opener (To attract the creature) ↗

Sleeping bags (In case we are stranded) ↓

"I don't like this. Even if we do manage to catch the creature, what are we going to do with it?" Violet said.

This was a good question and none of us knew the answer. I'd been concentrating on how to actually catch the yeti but it might be really difficult to keep such a big creature in a net for long.

Who would want to remove a scary, hairy, seven-foot-tall creature? I had a sudden moment of detective genius.

"Agatha Numpton wants the situation under control, so we'll call her and she can arrange to get the creature taken away," I said. "I'm sure it must be part of her job to do stuff like that."

All we need now is for the Spaghetti Yeti to show up.

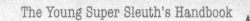

ESSENTIAL SKILLS: WILDERNESS TRACKING

The wilderness can be an unforgiving environment, but you may have to track suspects and look for clues there. A good detective has a range of outdoor detecting and survival skills they can call on in such situations.

Tips for Tracking a Suspect

Follow Their Trail: The edges of fresh footprints will look neat. If they are smudged, you may have a lot of catching up to do to find the suspect.

Fugitive

Follow Their Scent: Train your nose to recognise different perfumes and aftershaves. If you pick up a strong smell on the breeze it could lead you to your suspect.

Remember To Look Up: Don't just check at eye level. Whatever or whoever you are tracking could be hiding above you.

Tips for Building an Emergency Shelter:

A shower curtain provides protection from the elements. Why not wear a shower cap too? (Keeping your hair dry is a great way to avoid catching a cold.)

Cover your shelter with twigs and leaves to blend in with the undergrowth.

Use a tree trunk as a mystery pinboard.

TOP TIP

Practise building a shelter in your back garden before going into the wilderness.

WARNING

Always tell a responsible adult where you are going and make sure they know you could be away for some time. You don't want the emergency services turning up to rescue you just as you catch a criminal.

10:00PM
LIMPET LOUNGER CAFÉ, EMERGENCY
WILDLIFE WANDERER COLLECTION POINT

Unbelievable stuff has JUST happened!

As well as the Mystery Girls, Arthur and the
Peanut, four other kids showed up for the
Wildlife Wander. I should have been scared but
I was actually totally excited about our plan
to trap a real-life mystery creature.

As Jemima led us into the woods, it started
to rain. Me, Poppy and Violet hung back from
the group, scanning for signs of yeti activity
with our torches.

Violet grabbed my arm. "Something's
moving, over there," she breathed.

My heart thumped. I flashed my torch to where she was pointing, but it was just the wind making tree branches move around.

We walked deeper into the trees – the wind howled and the rain got heavier. At any moment the creature might get a whiff of the open tin of spaghetti Poppy was clutching and pounce on us. (Poppy was totally brave to act as bait.) It was really spooky. If Sally Gum in Totally Thrilling Mysteries were ever on a hunt for a wild creature, it would definitely be like this.

Not everyone thought it was so cool. A girl called Susan tripped over a tree root into a muddy puddle.

"I didn't even want to come! Mum just wanted me out of the way so she could finish her book!" she wailed.

"Liven up, Wanderers!" Jemima said. "This is a known squirrel hang-out! Shout NUTS if you spot any tracks!"

Everyone groaned and carried on trudging through the mud.

Suddenly, Arthur shouted, "NUTS!" and Jemima hurried over to inspect what he was looking at.

By this point, I was starting to worry that even wild rampaging spaghetti-loving yetis might look for shelter in this sort of weather – and that meant our plan wasn't going to work.

KABOOM!

Lightning flashed, followed by an enormous roll of thunder.

A boy called Errol screamed and Violet whimpered. But it wasn't the storm that bothered me. It was the expression on Jemima's face.

She was staring at Arthur's squirrel footprint. I peered over her shoulder and, even in the torchlight, I could tell that it definitely had not been made by a squirrel.

I called Poppy and Violet over. They stared at it too.

massive

We all held our breath and scanned the gloomy woods for movement with our torches. The yeti had been here – was it still close?

"Erm. It's probably from a ... a ..." Jemima said.

The woods lit up in another flash of lightning. It was only for a second, but it was long enough for us to see what was standing, half hidden by a bush, a few metres behind Jemima and Arthur...

"YEEEEETTTTIIIIIIII" shrieked the Peanut.

ARRRGGGGgggghhhhh!

I tried to stay calm because that's what detectives are supposed to do in these sorts of situations. As the rest of the Wanderers scattered, I reached into the mini-Mystery Kit and pulled out the net. It came out tangled in a big ball. No!

Lightning flashed again and I caught another glimpse of the creature, which was now taking jerky steps towards us, the rushing wind whipping up its long hair. Poppy dropped her tin of spaghetti and staggered back.

"RUN!" Violet screeched, trying to drag me away.

The creature's yellow eyes flickered like old broken light bulbs in a haunted house. I'd never seen anything like it. It was taller than a gorilla and hairier too, and those eyes were horrible. That's when fear took over, and I ran as fast as I could after the others.

11:10PM
MYSTERY GIRLS HQ, LISTENING TO THE STORM OUTSIDE

When the Wildlife Wanderers' parents showed up, they were NOT happy with Jake and Jemima. I'm sure it isn't going to take long for Agatha Numpton to hear about this. I keep wondering if it's bad enough to make her close the campsite. But I can't concentrate properly because all I can think about is those horrible flashing eyes.

Arghhh!

"What was I thinking? Letting you all go into the woods with that creature on the loose?" Mum said.

"I want to move to a caravan, where the yeti can't get me!" Arthur sobbed into Dad's shoulder.

"I'll use my pocket money to pay! Please can we do that?" Violet begged. (Violet! Honestly, the Peanut was holding it together better than she was.)

"This doesn't feel like much of a holiday. Perhaps we should just go home," Dad said, sighing.

For a horrible moment, Mum looked as if she was seriously considering it.

mum

Dad

"We can't!" I said. "You've put so much work into Sheep Fest, Mum. You can't cancel now."

Mum hesitated. "It's just an idea," she said. "Let's sleep on it." She put her arm around Arthur and led him and the Peanut to their tent.

I'm in my sleeping bag now, but there's NO WAY I'm sleeping, or going home tomorrow.

The Young Super Sleuth's Handbook says that after a scary situation you should focus your nervous energy* into planning your next move.

*NERVOUS ENERGY: When you are hyped up and will either scream hysterically or come up with an amazing idea.

FULL of
nervous
energy

"I know we've just had a totally terrifying experience, but the only way to save this campsite is to find some other way to stop that thing," I said.

"But you've seen it – there's no way we can catch it. It's too big – and too scary," Violet said.

We sat in silence as the storm raged outside. Then Poppy said,

"Well ... now that we know what we are dealing with, maybe we just need a bigger, better, yeti-sized trap. We could leave one in the woods, that way we don't have to face it again."

bigger trap

I like Poppy's thinking, and Violet does too. It just proves that the Mystery Girls never give up. First thing tomorrow, that's what we are going to do.

my determined
Face

Thursday 24th July

BAD NEWS ALERT: I knew she'd be back. We saw Agatha leaving the campsite office early this morning — Jake has told us that after last night, she has moved Limpet Rocks from an Official Warning to Being Under Threat of Closure. It's up to the Mystery Girls now!

arrghh!

11:00AM
LIMPET ROCKS WOODS, WOODLAND PATH
TO CAMPSITE

When people heard the details of
what happened last night, there
was a queue of cars lining
up to leave.

We heard a camper a few tents away saying
that Bay Bottom Holiday Park in town is almost
full and he needs to try and get in there before
it's too late.

It's so unfair. Jake and Jemima don't deserve to be shut down and lose all their customers because of some stupid yeti.

Some good news, though. At breakfast, Mum and Dad said we definitely won't be going home early.

"I don't like it, but I can't let the Sheep Fest organisers down at such short notice," Mum said. "My name would be mud in the knitting world."

It's been a busy morning. We searched the scene of last night's yeti sighting for evidence. Violet didn't want to go back into the woods, but I reminded her that the Spaghetti Yeti has never been active in daylight. (Even I would think twice about coming back if it had.)

The only thing we found
was the same massive footprint
Arthur spotted. I got really excited
thinking that if there were more
footprints nearby, we could follow
them and find the creature's hiding
place, but there was just that one.

"The others must have been washed away
by the rain," Violet said.

It seems a bit weird this one wasn't washed
away too, but I can't think of any other reason.
Anyway – our trap is set! I'm sure Arthur won't
miss his sleeping bag. We've laid it out on
the ground under some trees and put a plate
of spaghetti on top to act as bait. There are
spaghetti hoops, spaghetti shaped like pirates,
and tinned bolognese. (We raided the campsite
bins as campers have thrown away
all spaghetti-based products.)

Once the Spaghetti Yeti gets a whiff,
it won't be able to resist grabbing
the plate and scoffing the lot,
and when it does, a weight
will fall from the tree above
(Mystery Kit stuffed with
Totally Thrilling
Mystery books and
some of Arthur's
clothes), then the
sleeping bag will be
pulled upwards by
strands of Mum's wool
and the creature will be
trapped inside. Ha!

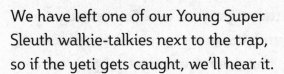

heavy
weight

sleeping bag
pulled up

We have left one of our Young Super
Sleuth walkie-talkies next to the trap,
so if the yeti gets caught, we'll hear it.

young
SUPER
SLEUTH

"Do you think it'll actually work?" said Poppy.

"Of course! The Young Super Sleuth's Handbook
hasn't failed us yet," I said. (We have studied the
trap-setting section carefully.)

"Well, we can't do anything until the yeti wakes up tonight," said Poppy. "Why don't we start our costumes for the parade tomorrow? I still can't believe that Olga woman wouldn't sell us that glitter wig."

Obsessed with glitter wigs

Glitter wigs and costumes don't seem very important but at least it will keep us busy until we face the yeti and save the campsite tonight. All in a day's work for the Mystery Girls!

(Poppy has decided we should dress up as the Fishy Four because her other designs won't work without glitter wigs. The Fishy Four mostly wear everyday stuff, but there is quite a bit of work to do making cool detective gadget props.)

DETECTIVE PROPS

Fishy four outfits

briefcase

7:00PM
CAMPSITE GATES, SCARY SITUATION
UNFOLDING!

We spent hours making Fishy Four props today, because Poppy thought our costumes would be rubbish without cardboard X-ray specs.

We were sitting outside Mystery HQ listening to the walkie-talkie for sounds of the yeti, when we heard a screech of tyres and car doors slamming at the front of the campsite.

Arthur and the Peanut squeaked. Mum and Dad barely looked up from their books. Me, Poppy and Violet rushed to see what was going on.

A TV news van had pulled up outside the gates, and a loud woman with swishy hair was in front of the Limpet Rocks sign, being filmed. Jake and Jemima were standing awkwardly next to her.

Rachel Smiley

"This is Rachel Smiley reporting. If you thought Salty Bay was a sleepy seaside town, you were wrong," Rachel Smiley was saying. "This is a town gripped by fear after a series of terrifying incidents involving a wild animal, known to locals as the Spaghetti Yeti – on this very campsite."

Rachel Smiley pointed her microphone at Jemima's face. "What do you propose to do about this dangerous animal? We've heard you don't care about the safety of your campers."

As Jemima struggled to answer, I glanced around. It wasn't just me, Violet and Poppy watching; a crowd of campers had gathered too.

There was more noise at the campsite gates and we saw Olga De Bouffet from Smoke and Mirrors marching towards the reception. Mr Roads from the rock shop was with her, as well as the moody Bay Bottom manager and loads of other shopkeepers from the town.

They were waving placards that said *Limpet Rocks Flops! The Yeti is a Threat-i* and *Save Salty Bay!* Bella the ice-cream lady was there as well – the stress from her yeti encounter on Monday must been too much for her, because she looked really upset.

Rachel Smiley's eyes lit up. "You're filming this, aren't you?" she shouted to her cameraman. She pointed her microphone to the crowd.

"First you steal all my customers, and now you let this yeti run riot in Salty Bay!" the manager of Bay Bottom shouted at Jake and Jemima. "We never had any problems here before you came!"

Olga took a step towards the camera. "You have made my life a misery and you don't care!" she shouted dramatically. "You haven't done anything about the hordes of children from your campsite causing chaos in my shop. It doesn't surprise me you aren't doing anything about this yeti problem either."

The manager of Bay Bottom cheered and waved his *No More Spaghetti Regret-i* placard. The other shopkeepers waved their placards too.

"I can't stay here – it's not safe! This place should be shut down!" Olga said, before bursting into totally fake tears.

She made sure that the cameraman got a close-up shot of her over-the-top blubbering before storming back down the hill into town. What a drama queen. It was the worst acting I'd ever seen.

Now everyone is complaining and arguing and it's all being filmed. Jake and Jemima look as if they'd quite like the yeti to come and carry them off into the woods. We need to stop this yeti once and for all!

9:10PM
LIMPET ROCKS WOODS

Finally, it looked as if Rachel Smiley and her crew
were going to pack up. Then...

"Arrrrgggggggghhhhhh!"

Horror!

Bella's

Bella had one hand clasped
to her mouth, the other
pointing towards the
woods. "THE YETI!" she
said, her voice trembling
with fear. "Over there!"

My eyes flashed to the treeline.
I couldn't see anything, but my heart was
racing. Why hadn't our trap worked? We'd left
loads of spaghetti – it should have been foolproof.

For a moment there was silence. Then – chaos.

"IT'S BACK!" screamed one camper.

"SPAGHETTI! HE'S EATING SPAGHETTI!" another woman yelled, pointing at a man who was eating something from a plastic plate. It did look like spaghetti. What was he thinking?

I felt Poppy grab my arm. She shoved the Young Super Sleuth walkie-talkie to my ear.

"It's in the trap," she breathed. "We've got it!"

I strained to hear over all the shouting. There was a scratching, swishing sound. And breathing. Something struggling. The creature must have run straight into our trap. Amazing! (It must move really quickly if Bella only saw it a few seconds ago.)

Wow. This is it. The Mystery Girls have caught the Spaghetti Yeti!

11:07PM
MYSTERY HQ

UNBELIEVABLENESS ALERT!

For the last few hours I have been living in a Totally Thrilling Mystery story. Sally Gum would be proud. (Except the Totally Thrilling Mystery stories never have completely disastrous endings where the detectives mess everything up.)

This would NEVER happen to the Fishy Four!

9:16PM: In the darkness of the wood, we can hear the distant panic at the campsite.

9:25PM: We reach the trap. Arthur's sleeping bag is wriggling around like a piece of electrified spaghetti. Is this the Spaghetti Yeti?

9:33PM: CRACK! A twig snaps. We turn around. We're not alone.

CRACK!

9:34PM: I catch a glimpse of dark fur in the undergrowth. Poppy gasps and Violet shouts, "TWO YETIS! RUN!"

9:35PM: A hairy creature staggers towards us from the shadows, its arms outstretched. My torch beam flashes across its face.

9:36PM: "Help us!" Arthur sobs. He falls at my feet, dressed in his monkey sleep suit. "Pippa said if we wanted to be proper detectives we had to find the yeti before you did. But she got caught in the trap!" A muffled cry comes from inside the sleeping bag.

ARTHUR

9:37PM: Poppy tells me to stop shouting at Arthur because if Pippa is in the trap then the yeti is still on the loose.

9:38PM: CRASH! CRACK! THUD! We all freeze. I quickly deduce that the only thing big enough to make a noise like that is the Spaghetti Yeti. "RUN!" Violet screams.

9:40PM: Ziiiiiiiiiip! I manage to free the Peanut and she falls to the ground just as a terrifying figure emerges from the bushes. GRRRrrrrrrr!

The Peanut

9:41PM: I shout at the Peanut to run, but she is frozen with fear, gazing at the looming shape of the Spaghetti Yeti approaching.

9:43PM: I sprint back to get the Peanut. My torch beam bounces over the trees, the leafy ground, the yeti's shimmering fur. Its yellow eyes flicker out of the darkness, fixing on me.

9:44PM: Now I'm close enough to hear the swish of the creature's fur. I grab at what I hope is Pippa and pull her arm. We run and don't look back.

MISSION UNSUCCESSFUL: SPAGHETTI YETI STILL LURKING IN THE WOODS.

11:45PM
MYSTERY HQ, UNABLE TO SLEEP

When we got back to camp Mum and Dad were really cross.

"We thought Arthur and Pippa were asleep in their tent – the next thing we know, you are all missing!" said Mum.

"We told you not to go into the woods at night, and you definitely shouldn't have taken Arthur and Pippa, especially not when you know there is a wild creature on the loose," Dad said.

annoyed

I was going to explain that that without us Half
a Mystery would totally be spaghetti on toast,
but then Poppy started shouting.

"She's got a glitter wig!" she said,
pointing at the Peanut, who was
clutching a shrivelled handful of
glittery strands. "She's bought
it to ruin our chances in the
competition!"

"It grabbed me, so I tried
to shake it off and ... and ... IT'S YETI FUR!"
the Peanut managed to croak.

"Right!" said Mum, cutting her off and glaring at
me, Poppy and Violet. "BEDTIME!"

Bedtime? Professional detectives do not get
sent to bed by their parents! Urgh. If the Peanut
and Arthur hadn't messed this whole thing up,
we'd be sitting round the campfire right now
explaining how we caught the Spaghetti Yeti
and solved the case.

"That's it," I said to Poppy and Violet when we were in our sleeping bags. "Agatha will definitely shut the campsite now. I feel like we've let Jake and Jemima down."

"Mariella, I hate to say this, but it might be for the best," said Violet. "The campsite isn't safe. That thing looked like it wanted to eat us more than it wanted spaghetti."

"Violet's right," said Poppy. I knew it was serious because Poppy NEVER agrees with Violet about stuff like this.

Nobody said anything for a while. I'd usually reply that they were both wrong and the Mystery Girls can handle anything, but I'd run out of ideas.

stumped

scared

in shock

"Shimmering fur. And those yellow eyes," I said. "It's like a monster from a bad dream."

Bad dream

Poppy and Violet didn't answer. They have fallen asleep! How is that even possible? This isn't how it works out in Totally Thrilling Mysteries. Sally Gum always knows what to do. Though I suppose nobody would buy the books if they had rubbish endings like this.

THE UNSOLVED MYSTERY

Even though you have followed correct procedure, you may find yourself in the embarrassing situation of having an unsolved mystery. It's essential to know what to do if this happens.

Quick Fixes for Unsolved Mysteries:

Check food wasn't spilled on witness statements. This can conceal vital case-solving clues.

Egg?

Taking a break can often help you to see things more clearly. Why not do some stretches?

Is poor eyesight causing you to miss clues?

Have your parents hoovered up important evidence while cleaning Mystery HQ?

I have caught the suspect!

Discovering Famous Detectives:
The Ruined Career of Hetty Winkwell

Hetty Winkwell was a well-respected
detective until she monumentally messed
up The Case of the Apple Tart Terroriser.

Hetty had become relaxed after solving every
case she'd ever investigated. But after the
bakery she was keeping under surveillance was raided
while Hetty casually took
a break to have a shampoo and set,
nobody wanted to hire her any
more. She turned to a life of crime,
sabotaging other detectives to destroy
their reputations like she
had destroyed her own.

WARNING

If you leave a series of mysteries unsolved,
you are probably not cut out for detective
work and may be ruining the good name
of the Young Super Sleuth's
Handbook. Call our
hotline for advice.

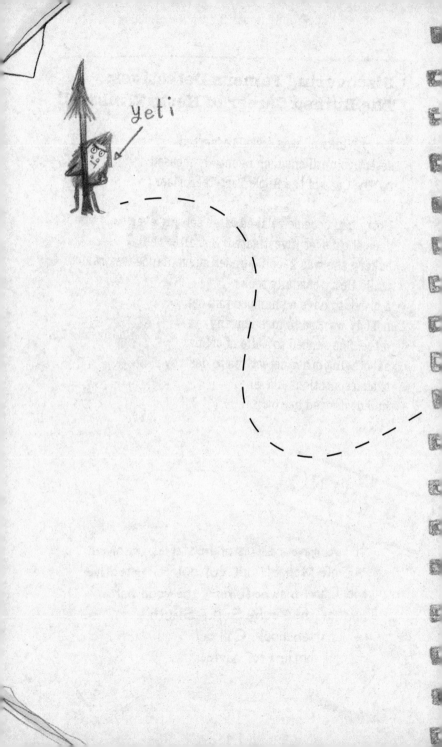

Yeti

my totally shocked face

1:06AM
MYSTERY HQ

BREAKTHROUGH ALERT!

I couldn't sleep so I've been reading one of my Totally Thrilling Mystery books – *The Monster of Mulberry Manor*. It's all about the Fishy Four investigating reports of a terrifying creature that appears in the corridors of a spooky old seaside hotel. Just like this holiday.

But *The Monster of Mulberry Manor* has an unexpected twist. For ages you are waiting for the Fishy Four to catch the monster, then Sally Gum makes an amazing breakthrough.

Totally Thrilling Mysteries

Sally's torch flashed around the cellar over stacks of boxes and old bed frames. Poking out from under the lid of an old trunk was ... a familiar hairy purple arm.

Sally staggered backwards. The monster was here. Hang on, she thought. Why was its arm so still? So ... flat?

"Fish sticks! There's something fishy going on here!" said Sally, flinging open the trunk.

Scrunched inside was the monster, its evil eyes staring up at her.

"It's a costume! Somebody has been wearing a monster costume to scare everyone!" Sally gasped in the darkness.

UTTERY SHOCKING REALISATION: What if the Spaghetti Yeti isn't a yeti at all? What if it's ... a PERSON?

I didn't see it at first, but there is even evidence! The glitter strands the Peanut had, and when my torch shone on the fur, it shimmered. I don't know much about yetis, but I'm pretty sure they've never been described as having glittery fur.

Disco yeti

And a motive! Salty Bay was like a ghost town compared to how busy the campsite was when we arrived. If this place closes, it would make a lot of shop owners very happy. Now I think about it, this case has all the signs of sabotage!*

*SABOTAGE: When a person deliberately makes things go wrong to get revenge, or to get their own way.

8:45AM
LIMPET ROCKS WOODS, NEXT TO
ABANDONED YETI TRAP

I couldn't wake Poppy and Violet last night.
Violet kept talking in her sleep: "I'm not a piece
of spaghetti, please don't eat meeee!" And Poppy
told me to get lost and pulled her pillow over her
head. But this morning I finally got enough sense
out of them to share my fake yeti theory.

"The locals don't like Limpet Rocks,
but would one of them really go
to the trouble of dressing up as
a fake yeti to get it shut
down?" said Violet. "That
thing in the woods looked
real to me. Maybe Pippa just
found the glitter on the floor?"

shocked!

But that still
doesn't explain the
shimmery fur, or the
flickering eyes.

"It can't be. I know
loads about costumes.
I'm sure I would have spotted
a fake," Poppy said.

WEIRD

"That's the problem, Poppy. We thought the yeti
was real so we haven't been looking for the right
sorts of things! We need to examine everything
in a completely new light," I said.

We've decided the most logical place to start
looking for evidence to back up the fake yeti
theory is the scene of last night's attack. I'm
relieved we've found something useful because
the campsite really is in trouble. There are only
about twenty tents left. Dad says he's heard
those campers are only still here because Bay
Bottom Holiday Park is officially full. Arthur
and the Peanut are refusing to go anywhere
without Mum.

EVIDENCE THE YETI IS FAKE

ANOTHER MASSIVE FOOTPRINT:

Just one, next to our yeti trap.
Why is there only ONE? It's
the same as the one we saw on
the Wildlife Wander. The creature
did not look as if it hopped on
one leg. Could this have been made
deliberately by somebody?

GLITTER WIG: More strands of what
looks like glitter wig on the ground
and in tree branches.

HAIR PINS: Found near the glitter
wig strands. Wild animals do not
usually take the time to style their
hair. Humans do, though, especially
female ones.

VERDICT: There is sufficient evidence
to follow a new line of enquiry — that the
yeti is not what it seems. We are turning
our attentions to look for a person instead
of a wild mythical creature. But who?

10:00AM
LIMPET ROCKS DECKCHAIR AREA, SUSPECT PROFILING COMPLETE

Our list of suspects is quite long – it's basically anyone who owns a shop in Salty Bay. The Young Super Sleuth's Handbook says if you want to narrow your list of potential suspects, then making a suspect profile is a good idea, so that's what we have done.

LIKELY CHARACTERISTICS OF SOMEBODY WHO WOULD PRETEND TO BE A SPAGHETTI YETI:

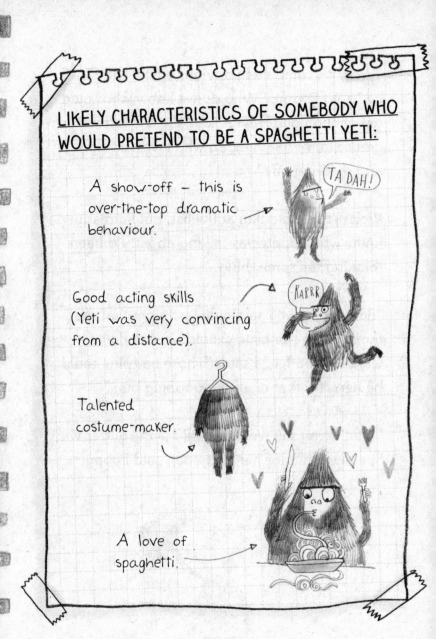

A show-off — this is over-the-top dramatic behaviour.

Good acting skills (Yeti was very convincing from a distance).

Talented costume-maker.

A love of spaghetti.

"Well, it's completely obvious who it MUST be," said Poppy. "Who do we know who could get enough glitter wigs to make a massive yeti costume? Somebody who loves acting and showing off?"

Violet stared blankly at the list, but I already knew who Poppy was talking about. I'd been thinking the same thing.

"Somebody who said only last night that she thought the campsite should be shut down – Olga De Bouffet," I said. "Those hairpins could be hers, for that eyebrow-popping bun."

"That's why she wouldn't sell me the glitter wig! She needed it for her costume," said Poppy.

THE YETI?

wig

Poppy was totally
angry about the glitter
wig incident and it did
make me wonder if we
were letting how horrible
Olga had been to us get
in the way of considering
other suspects. The owner
of Bay Bottom had been shouting
stuff at the protest last night too, and he was
doing really well now Limpet Rocks was in so
much trouble. But why would he have hairpins?

FUMING

But when I think about Olga's fake upset
performance last night, my Mystery Senses
tell me that she is the only one of the shop
owners capable of doing something as
unhinged as dressing up
in a fake yeti costume.

CRAZY

"All of the shop owners were here last night when the yeti was spotted," said Violet. "So how could it be any of them?"

It was good Violet was thinking things through, but she was forgetting one other massive incriminating thing about Olga.

"Olga stormed off, remember? She could have got changed and then appeared in the trees!" Poppy said.

storming off

"You're right. Olga fits the profile and I'm sure it's her. But without something more concrete, all we have is a strong suspicion," I said.

"We need to be certain about this," said Violet. "What about Bella? Her hair is always pinned in crazy styles so those hairpins could be hers."

"But it was her who saw the yeti," Poppy said. "And she's not stuck in boring old Salty Bay town with no customers. She said so herself. With her van she can sell ice-cream anywhere."

Everything so far points to Olga but the Young Super Sleuth's Handbook says you shouldn't go round accusing people without knowing for sure.

"We need to visit Smoke and Mirrors. There could be some incriminating evidence there," Poppy said.

It's a good idea, but it won't be easy. I doubt Olga keeps her yeti outfit with the other animal costumes – if she's masterminded this crazy plan, she'll be far too sneaky for that. Well, the Mystery Girls will just have to be even sneakier.

THE CUNNING CRIMINAL: THE MASTER OF DISGUISE

Criminals often disguise their true identity so they can avoid the finger of blame being pointed at them.
Do you have what it takes to unmask a criminal master of disguise or will you be fooled by their trickery?

True identity concealed

Levels of Disguise Deception:

1. Mild Misconception
Carefully-selected every day clothing used to blend in and look as innocent as possible while committing a crime.

Stolen money

2. Total Trickery
A more elaborate disguise – dressing in fake uniforms and wearing fake beards, glasses or prosthetic noses.

Fake nose and facial hair

3. Dastardly Deception
The most sophisticated form of disguise – criminals may dress as weird objects or animals. Such costumes are used to secretly gain entry to premises, to scare people away or to deliberately create hysteria.

Animal or human?

Disguises Used by Real Criminals:

The Post Box Pincher:
Spent years pickpocketing
innocent pedestrians who
thought they were just walking
past a normal post box.

**The Masterpiece
Mastermind:** Stole priceless
works of art while posing as
a sculpture in museums.

The Terrible Tooth Fairy:
This dentist sabotaged a rival
surgery by appearing in their
waiting room dressed as an
evil tooth-stealing fairy.

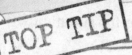

TOP TIP

Why not play criminals at
their own game and become a
master of disguise yourself?
Make sure your collection
of disguises is kept up
to date and well organised.

Dolphin

12:10PM
HIDING BEHIND DOLPHIN STATUE,
OUTSIDE SMOKE AND MIRRORS

We've decided that Poppy should be the one to go in. She's a brilliant actor and always puts a lot of emotion into her synchronised swimming performances.

Me and Violet will be following Olga's one-child-at-a-time rule by staying outside. Other tourists will think we've just stopped to admire the sea view, but we'll really be monitoring the situation closely through the window.

I'm not sure what we're expecting to find – maybe some designs for the fake yeti or a pinboard with pictures of yetis all over it. Or stolen spaghetti from the campsite. (Was Olga eating it so she had the energy to run round at night scaring people?) If we can find something to prove she's been faking the yeti, we'll have a chance of saving the campsite.

Hang on ... CLUE ALERT!

The troll dummy in the window is missing one of his big hairy feet! A big hairy yeti-sized foot, and two random footprints in the woods? This is too much of a coincidence not to be related!

"Look!" I whispered to Poppy and Violet. "That troll's foot is the perfect size to have made one of those fake yeti footprints we've seen!"

"She's not getting away with this!" Poppy said. "I'm going in!"

hiding

12:45PM
ALLEYWAY, HIDING BETWEEN ROCKY ROADS'
ROCK SHOP AND THE COCONUT SHACK

Wow. We've just escaped from Olga. It was like
being in a Totally Thrilling Mysteries chase scene,
and there was an unexpected outcome from
Poppy's mission.

CASE REPORT: POPPY HOLMES, UNDERCOVER MYSTERY SHOPPER

12:15PM: Poppy enters Smoke and Mirrors like a normal carefree customer. Olga immediately pokes her head out from the back of the shop.

casual

12:16PM: Poppy pretends to look at costumes. Really she is looking for yeti-related evidence. She asks Olga if her next delivery of glitter wigs has arrived yet.

12:17PM: Olga tells Poppy they have already sold and that she's sure this will be the last EVER costume parade because she heard on Bay News that the campsite is about to be shut down. Olga chuckles to herself, not even bothering to hide that she's happy about it.

12:18PM: Poppy conceals her anger and asks who bought the glitter wigs. It seems strange somebody would want so many of them.

137

12:19PM: Olga glares at Poppy. Poppy remembers her Mystery Girl training and deflects suspicion by using flattery. She says she's only interested in the glitter wigs because one day she'd love to be on the stage, just like Olga.

12:20PM: Olga pauses to tidy her wig display. Poppy suspects Olga is trying to think up an excuse because really she has used all the glitter wigs herself for the yeti costume.

CIRCUS

wigs

12:21PM: Olga says that Bella Gelato bought the wigs because Bella loves crazy costumes after spending years as part of the old Gelato Family Circus before it shut down.

SOLD

Bella?

12:23PM: It's the worst excuse Poppy has ever heard. She looks at some fake moustaches until Olga tells her that if she isn't buying anything she should get out.

moustaches

12:24PM: Poppy needs more time to find evidence. She stalls by saying the first thing that comes into her head and asks Olga if she sells big plastic trolls' feet.

12:26PM: Anger flashes over Olga's face. Poppy's heart thuds. Has Olga guessed the real reason Poppy is asking? Olga screams at Poppy, "YOU! It was you who stole that troll's foot out of my window!"

12:27PM: Poppy aborts the mission and sprints out of the shop. Olga chases after us all like a wild rampaging yeti.

VERDICT: Poppy thinks Olga was covering her tracks by making up that stuff up about Bella being in the circus and the troll's foot being stolen. She also thinks that comment Olga made about the costume parade is totally suspicious. Is she planning to come back as the yeti tonight? She looks totally guilty but unfortunately we still have no actual concrete evidence that she is the Spaghetti Yeti.

Hardly any tents   Abandoned deckchairs

1:00PM
LIMPET ROCKS CAMPSITE WALL,
PLANNING NEXT STEPS

Back at the campsite Jake and Jemima were
setting up for the costume parade. They told
us the only reason it's still happening is because
when Agatha saw last night's news footage,
the cameras somehow hadn't spotted the yeti.

Agatha usually needs a confirmed sighting to
issue the Notice of Closure but she has now
written a new rule saying that from
today a confirmed sighting will
no longer be necessary. If there is
one more sniff of the yeti she can
INSTANTLY close the campsite!

SALTY
BAY
RULE
BOOK
by Agatha Overton

I was pleased we'd have time to prove that Olga is really the yeti, but also had a weird niggling feeling. Olga's story about Bella being a circus performer was a strange thing to just make up.

"Could Olga have been telling the truth about Bella buying the glitter wigs and the foot being stolen?" I said.

"No way," said Poppy. "She's just covering her tracks."

"Yeah," said Violet. "We all saw how scared Bella was when she told us about her attack, and she was the one who spotted the yeti last night."

That must be it. Of course Olga would lie to lead us away from her. She is a master of disguise. When she comes back tonight, the Mystery Girls will be waiting!

2:40PM
OUTSIDE CAMPSITE GATES, STUNNED.

HUGE BREAKTHROUGH ALERT!
(I don't think I can cope with any more.)

We were sitting on the campsite wall, trying
to come up with a plan to catch Olga tonight
when we heard the cheerful chimes of Bella's
ice-cream van.

TUM tum TE TUM, TUM TUM TE TUMMMM Te TUM TUM.

"Hello, girls, you look as if you need an ice-cream," Bella said, pulling up next to us.

"Amazing! That's exactly what we need," Violet said. "Thanks, Bella!"

For a moment, the idea of sitting in the sunshine eating an ice-cream made everything seem normal – not at all like we've got to somehow stop a crazy yeti-woman by the end of the evening. Me and Violet chose raspberry ripple.

"Pink Fizz ice lolly, please," said Poppy.

pink
FIZZ

Bella smiled as she passed me and Violet our ice creams, then she turned to get Poppy's ice lolly.

"Good choice," she said, struggling to open the freezer. "I'm partial to a pink fizz myself."

It was then that I noticed
something strange stuck to
the freezer's sliding lid.
Something shiny.

As Bella threw her body
weight into trying to get
the lid to budge, a silver
strand wiggled like piece
of sparkling spaghetti.
There was no mistaking.
It was a bit of glitter wig.

A glance to my left told me Poppy and Violet
had seen it too.

With one last heave, Bella slid the lid open and
leaned inside the freezer. I stood on my tiptoes
to try and see what that strand was attached to.
A heap of tangled glitter wigs twinkled under
boxes of lollies. The yeti costume!

I just about managed to fix the expression on my face before Bella turned around.

"There we go! Pink Fizz!" she said, passing the lolly to Poppy. "Now, girls, you will be careful at that costume parade tonight, won't you? I don't know what those people are thinking, holding a parade at a time like this – with a wild yeti lurking in the woods."

"Will do," I managed to say before we backed away into the campsite.

TUM tum TE TUM, TUM TUM TE TUMMMM Te TUM TUM.

The van's chimes sounded different as Bella drove off. Now we know there's a yeti costume in her freezer, the happy song seemed distinctly sinister.

Serious
↓

3:30PM
SITTING ON ABANDONED DECKCHAIRS,
FIGURING OUT NEXT STEPS

I can't believe we have been so easily fooled –
a yeti, a crazy fancy-dress shop owner, and now
it turns out the Spaghetti Yeti is actually an ice-
cream lady in a weird costume. I should know
better – this isn't the first time somebody in an
investigation has seemed perfectly nice but has
actually been a crazed criminal.

"Shouldn't we just tell Agatha that the yeti is
fake?" said Violet.

I wish stopping Bella was going to be that simple.
But we only have one option to untangle this
mess of yeti spaghetti.

"Think about how that sounds, Violet. Agatha will just think we are silly kids," I said. "Even if we had the glitter wig costume, who will believe it was actually the scary creature in the woods? It won't be easy but our only option is to catch Bella in the act, tonight."

"Urgh! That woman! It's such a HORRIBLE thing to do. People have been terrified!" Poppy said. "I wish I could sneak up on her in a big scary costume. See how she likes it."

PING! Poppy had just given me an amazing idea. We are going to need some new costumes!

**5:06PM
MYSTERY GIRLS HQ,
COSTUME PRODUCTION CENTRE**

We have told Mum and Dad and Arthur and
the Peanut that they are not to disturb us this
afternoon because we are putting top-secret
finishing touches to our costumes for the parade.
We are making completely new ones to spook
Bella with. If everything goes according to plan,
she'll run, terrified, from the woods onto
the campsite and be unmasked as the
great big fake yeti she really is! HA!

seaweed

"Who needs glitter wigs? Seaweed looks much more like yeti fur," Poppy said. "We might even be able to wrap this up and get back for the parade judging. I'm sure these could be a winner!"

(Well, if anyone can solve this mystery and win a costume parade, it's the Mystery Girls.)

Violet found some perfect spooky accessories in the Sparkling Starfish Souvenir Shop – glow-in-the-dark bouncy balls that we've turned into yeti eyeballs.

"Wow! That's horrible – I can't look at you!" Violet said, when Poppy tried on one of the costumes.

It really did look scary. If Poppy caught me by surprise in some dark woods I'd totally scream and run off. Now we just have to hope that Bella will do the same!

8:00PM
LIMPET ROCKS CAMPSITE, COSTUME PARADE PARTY. POW-WOW AREA, NEXT TO BUFFET TABLE

No sign of Bella Gelato or her stupid glitter wig yeti. Not yet-i, anyway.

Jake and Jemima are doing their best to be cheerful, but no amount of twinkly fairy lights and happy music are going to turn this into a party. People want them to hurry up and get to the parade bit so they can go and hide in their tents, but Jake says that they never do the judging until the party is in full swing.

Jake

Jemima

I've just seen a family dressed as oysters jump out of their skin because Arthur knocked into the hay bale that they are
sitting on. (He is dressed as mermaid, which looks quite odd.) And most parties don't have a Safety Officer inspecting the buffet table or a TV news crew outside the gates poised to film yeti activity.

Our yeti costumes are hidden in the Mystery Kit. For now we are dressed in our Fishy Four outfits. (Mum did say she couldn't wait to see the 'top secret' part of our costumes that we'd been working on all afternoon. Hmmm.)

Mum and Dad have said that after last night are we under no circumstances allowed to leave their sight after dark. We are waiting for some sort of distraction so we can escape to the woods and look for Bella.

8:50PM
JUST BEYOND TREELINE, LIMPET ROCKS WOODS

We are back in the woods again – but things are not going to plan.

At the campsite, the happy disco music only seemed to make it more obvious how none of the campers were really talking, but just nervously looking around, waiting for something to happen. Then –

RAAARrrrrARRRRR!

stunned

Poppy dropped her hot
dog and Violet shrieked.
The family of oysters hid
behind the buffet table.

Arthur's blue wig whipped
past my face as he ran
round waving his arms
and screaming. Agatha scribbled
gleefully on her clipboard before
leaping behind a hay bale.

Everyone dashing to find cover
gave us the perfect opportunity
to run for the treeline without
Mum and Dad noticing. I glanced
up to see birds flying out of the trees
squawking, as if they'd been disturbed by
something huge. How was Bella even doing that?
We were about to find out.

violet

Our race to try and unmask the yeti was fast-paced and totally scary. This is an accurate account of what happened and when. Read on if you dare.

Operation Finish a Fake Yeti

Poppy

me

8:55PM
LIMPET ROCKS WOODS, TRACKING FAKE SPAGHETTI YETI

I knew the yeti must be a fake, but those growls were still making my heart beat faster. As we sped along the woodland path, the sounds of panic from the campsite grew fainter, and the roaring grew louder.

RAARrrrrARRRRR!

"What if being a fake yeti wasn't enough? What if she's set a real one free?" Violet said, her eyes darting around the woods, as if something might leap out at any moment.

"This is a trick to scare people – it has to be," I said.

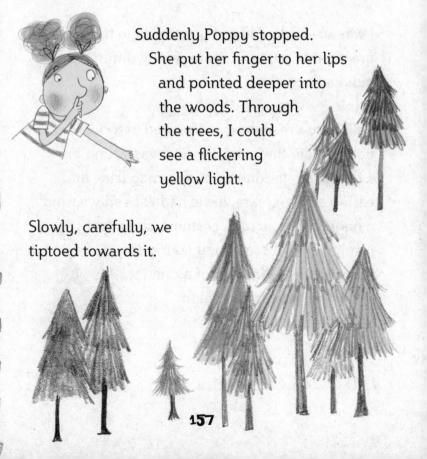

Suddenly Poppy stopped. She put her finger to her lips and pointed deeper into the woods. Through the trees, I could see a flickering yellow light.

Slowly, carefully, we tiptoed towards it.

9:10PM
LIMPET ROCKS WOODS, HIDDEN
IN BUSHES. SUSPECT LOCATED

I was so shocked I hardly noticed the twigs
poking into my bum as we watched from our
hiding place.

Bella's ice-cream van was parked in a clearing
not far from the campsite. She was sitting in
a deckchair, flicking through a magazine and
eating an ice-cream. If she hadn't been wearing
a huge, glittering yeti costume, she might
just have been somebody taking a
relaxing break, instead of a criminal
masterminding a campaign
of yeti terror.

The huge yeti head was on the ground next to her, its stick-on eyes staring blankly in our direction.

totally relaxed

Every so often, without bothering to raise her eyes from her magazine, Bella lifted a microphone to her mouth.

"**RAAAA**eeeeea**RrrrrARRR!**" she yelled.

The growl was being played at top volume through the speakers on the roof of the van. Bella chuckled to herself each time she did it. She really didn't care whose holiday she was ruining.

I peered closer. Strapped to her legs was a pair of long wooden poles.

"Stilts!" I whispered. "That's how she made the yeti look so tall."

Bella might have got away with crazy stunts in the circus, but she wasn't getting away with anything else while the Mystery Girls were around.

It took all of my willpower not to run from the bushes, screaming, "WE'RE ON TO YOU, YETI-WOMAN!" But the Young Super Sleuth's Handbook says that being a good detective isn't always about confronting the suspect in a dramatic showdown; it's about outwitting them.

When Bella finally stood on her stilts and got ready to move, we slid into our yeti costumes. It was time to put our plan into action.

Totally
FAKE!

9:20PM
LIMPET ROCKS WOODS, YETI STALKING

It was weird seeing Poppy and Violet in their yeti costumes, their bouncy-ball eyes glowing through the mist rising from the woodland floor. Even weirder was the noise Poppy made.

Grrrrr. **Garrrrraaaaggghh. Grrrrrr!**

The sound travelled in the still of the woods. Peeking out from our hiding place, I saw Bella look around. This was too good an opportunity to miss.

"**Grrr. Garrraaaggghh. Grrrrr,**" I croaked.

Bella was scanning the woods now, confused.

Poppy launched herself out of the
bushes and across the path,
black seaweed flying behind
her. Bella must have
only caught a glimpse,
but from inside her yeti
costume she let out a little
squeak.

It was working! Bella was spooked.

"Grrr. Garrraaaaggghh. Grrrr!"
I called. (I made it sound as weird
as possible.)

I darted across the path like
Poppy had done. Violet grabbed
my arm and got pulled along.

"Arrgghhheeeeaaahhhhhh!" she cried. (I think
this was genuine fear rather than her making an
actual fake yeti noise.)

At the sight of two weird creatures in front of her, Bella squeaked again. She wobbled on her stilts.

Poppy was slowly rising from the ground. Her head drooped down to one side, a bit like a zombie. In a sudden movement, she jerked her arms and head up and stared right at Bella. (Wow! Poppy is such a good actor.) Then she jumped forwards.

"Ahhheeeeeaaaa**rrr**hhhhh!**"** Bella screamed.

Me and Violet followed Poppy, making the same jerky movements. Who knows if that's the sort of thing a yeti would do – as long as it was scaring Bella, I didn't care. And it definitely was, because Bella turned and ran – straight down the path to the campsite!

9:40PM
LIMPET ROCKS CAMPSITE, YETI INVASION

We raced after Bella as she burst out from the trees and ran straight for the campsite pow-wow area, where the campers were still wandering around in fancy dress.

The TV crew were filming Agatha Numpton, who was waving a signed Notice of Closure at Jake and Jemima, wearing a smug expression on her face.

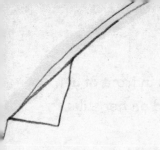

It was Arthur who spotted us first.

"YEEEeeeeTTTTIiiiiiiis!" he screamed.

After that it all happened
really quickly. Bella glanced
behind – big mistake –
her stilt clipped a tent
peg and sent her flying
through the air,
glittery fur
and all.

THUD!

She landed face down on the grass, a few steps
from the stunned campers.

Me, Poppy and Violet came to a stop just behind
her, too out of breath to speak.

The cameraman fixed his lens on Bella. The more
she struggled to get up, the more tangled and
twisted her costume became. Everyone looked
shocked. I whipped off the head of my costume.
Violet and Poppy did the same. It was time to
confront Bella Gelato.

"RAAAARrrrr!" Bella growled weakly.

"WHAT is the meaning of this?" said Agatha Numpton.

It was the perfect opportunity to explain exactly what had been going on. (I love this part of being a detective.) It felt totally amazing to be able to tell everyone they didn't need to live in terror of the rampaging yeti any more. YAY!

"There is NO yeti," I said. "Just an elaborate costume. The creature you see before you is Bella Gelato!"

The crowd gasped.

Bella made one final
attempt to get up, but all
that happened was that
the yeti head rolled off,
coming to a standstill at
Jemima's feet.

Shocked

There were a few squeals and shrieks.
It did look pretty weird seeing Bella's round
face and whipped-up ice-cream hair on top of
massive glittery fake yeti shoulders.

"What are you all looking at?" Bella snapped.
"They drove me to this." She was pointing at Jake
and Jemima. "They've stolen all my customers
with their stupid baked bean ice-cream parlour!"

Then she started having some sort of weird
yeti tantrum, kicking her stilts and wriggling
uselessly.

huge →
tantrum

Agatha flung her clipboard to the ground.
"This has been a complete waste of my time!
Do you have any idea how much paperwork will
be involved in retracting this Notice of Closure?"
she shouted.

"The campsite is safe, and still open for
business!" Jake beamed. "Thanks to the Mystery
Girls, you can all start enjoying your holidays
again!"

The crowd cheered. Me, Poppy and Violet
high-fived everyone. Three half-Mystery Girls,
half-yetis celebrating looked pretty strange,
but no stranger than a campsite full of dazed
campers in fancy dress and a yeti woman in
a massive sulk.

We'd done it. The Mystery Girls had solved the
most Totally Thrilling Mystery ever!

solved
the case
face →

Saturday 26th July

me relaxing

chilled

me, relaxing with an ice-cream

5:00PM
IN THE SEA, ON INFLATABLE LILO, SALTY BAY

We had to wait with Bella until
the Salty Bay police turned up.
She was furious, screaming that
Jake and Jemima should be arrested,
not her, for 'crimes against ice-cream'.

beans

The police said impersonating a yeti wasn't
something they'd ever dealt with before and
that, although serious, may just mean Bella
faces the embarrassment of everyone knowing
what she's done. The footage of Bella's yeti head
rolling along the ground has been played over
and over on the local news. It's totally the most
embarrassing thing ever so maybe the police
are right.

This morning, when Bella had calmed down, she issued a statement to the press apologising and saying that she isn't really a monster, she was just driven to act like one because she was so worried about her business.

Jake and Jemima are being very understanding. They told Rachel Smiley in an exclusive interview that Limpet Rocks Campsite would do its best from now on to send campers to the wonderful shops in Salty Bay. They have decided that running all the shops as well as the campsite is just too much hard work, and they also want to make sure that nothing like this happens EVER again.

The Spaghetti Yeti story has actually been a brilliant thing for Salty Bay. The local scenery shown on the news coverage looked so stunning that people have been making bookings at Limpet Rocks *and* Bay Bottom Holiday Park. They are both full up for the rest of the summer holidays!

stunning!

After we revealed Bella as the yeti last night, the party atmosphere was wild. Everyone was dancing and laughing and joking. We ended up doing a conga line round the campsite until 1am. Yay! Mum said she didn't know how she was going to concentrate on her knitting workshop at Sheep Fest after such a crazy evening, and such a late night.

peanut

We even got the cherry on the mystery-solving ice cream! The Mystery Girls were placed first in the fancy-dress competition. Poppy wdeserved it after pulling off such an amazing performance back in the woods and we are, after all, masters of disguise!

Everyone has been asking how we solved the case and figured out the yeti wasn't a yeti after all. Here is our case report in full:

CASE REPORT: THE SPAGHETTI YETI, SOLVED BY THE MYSTERY GIRLS

Bella Gelato had a simple motive – to close down Limpet Rocks along with its rival ice-cream parlour, Chill Your Beans. She was furious that Jake and Jemima had opened it so near to her own ice-cream parlour, Bella's.

Bella's family circus closed years previously because it lost all its customers to a rival. Bella had vowed never to let that happen again.

Bella's special skill from her circus days was stilt-walking, which she used on the campsite with terrifying effects. Thanks to these, and the costume she'd cleverly made from Olga De Bouffet's glitter wigs, witnesses were convinced they were the target of a seven-foot yeti.

stilts →

The first night Bella appeared as the yeti, she couldn't resist stealing spaghetti. (Bella's family is Italian and it's always been her favourite food.) When she heard that people had been referring to her as the Spaghetti Yeti, she decided to carry on doing it.

Bella tipped off the Salty Bay Safety Officer, Agatha Numpton and made Jake and Jemima look bad by ensuring that Bay News covered the dramatic and totally false story.

What gave Bella away was her shoddy approach to costume-making. She created her costume from 57 glitter wigs, sellotape and light-up googly eyes purchased from Smoke and Mirrors theatrical supplies shop.

(Bella also stole a plastic troll's foot from the shop window, which Olga had refused to sell her because it was a display item, to make huge fake footprints.)

The costume looked effective from a distance, but up close it was clearly fake. It also fell apart easily. After finding glitter wig strands in various locations, the Mystery Girls were highly suspicious.

They finally uncovered concrete evidence that the Spaghetti Yeti was a fake when they spotted the yeti costume hidden inside the freezer of Bella's ice-cream van.

Jake and Jemima have now closed Chill Your Beans! and have kindly offered Bella the chance to sell ice-cream at the end of their new Woodland Yeti Walk. (If only Bella had realised that talking to Jake and Jemima was the solution to her problem instead of running around dressed as a fake yeti.)

If you suspect yetis may be active in your area, we would urge you to contact the Mystery Girls immediately. We are now experts in spotting fakes but would still like to find a genuine legendary creature, like a yeti, one day.

CASE CLOSED.

NOTE: If your mystery is urgent, we are officially on holiday for the next couple of days, but will get back to you when we return.

The mystery Girls

Read on for a peek of
the next book in the
Mariella Mystery series:
A Kitty Calamity!

**Sunday
19th April**

watson

7:00PM
MYSTERY GIRLS HQ, TREE HOUSE IN MY BACK GARDEN

It's important to take every mystery situation seriously. That's why I totally can't be blamed for what just happened.

CASE REVIEW

THE NOWHERE-TO-BE-SEEN KITTY-NEXT-DOOR

Henry

Henry →

Ginger and currently Missing
Cat of our distraught next-door neighbour,
Josie Jones. Hasn't come home for
three days. We've searched everywhere
for him. Last seen wearing a glittery
red collar. Josie
(neighbour) →

MYSTERY GIRL INVESTIGATORS:

Violet Maple

Allergic to everything - including cats - but that doesn't stop her being an amazing detective.

Violet

Poppy Holmes

POPPY in a Sherlock Holmes hat

We thought she might be related to Sherlock Holmes (world-famous detective) because she is so good at finding clues, but then found out Sherlock Holmes is a made-up person in a book. Oh well. Poppy is still a talented Mystery Girl and synchronised swimmer.

Sherlock Holmes

Me and Watson 🐾

Mariella Mystery

I'm not sure Henry's disappearance is going to make us famous detectives, because when cats go missing it's usually because they are stuck up trees or have found a new owner who feeds them tastier food. There aren't any more complicated mysteries happening at the moment, though, so we've agreed to take on the case. (Also I'd be totally upset if Watson, trusty sidekick and pet cat, disappeared.)

CASE REVIEW MEETING GETS MYSTERIOUS

5:50PM: In HQ, Poppy has totally distracted me and Violet by using Watson as a model for our new set of detective fake moustaches.

moustaches →

cute

5:55PM: A piercing scream from outside HQ makes us all jump. Watson hides under the Mystery Desk.

spooked

5:56PM: The screamer is quickly identified. Arthur is standing under the tree house shouting hysterically "stuck in tree" and "fluffy".

screamer

5:58PM: Looking up through the leaves above HQ, there is a flash of ginger fur. Henry! I can't believe he has been here all the time. I launch a tree-scaling rescue attempt.

6:02PM: Gripping the tree with one hand, I reach towards Henry's bum, which is poking through the leaves.

FURRY BUM!

6:03PM: I realise the fluffy orange thing is most definitely *NOT* Henry. I have just risked everything to rescue... Arthur's fluffy kitten slipper.

FLuffy kitten slipper!

6:04PM: Josie from next door comes out of her house just as I'm flinging the slipper at Arthur's head. She also mistakes the slipper for Henry and shrieks. (Honestly, as if I'd fling the real Henry at Arthur's head.) Watson, distressed by all the noise, bolts from HQ, still wearing the fake moustache.

6:05PM: Mum comes outside. She sees me in the tree and shouts at me to get down. I can't. I am stuck.

6:45PM: Dad arrives home from work and I, elite Mystery Girl, have to be rescued from the tree while everyone watches. It's completely embarrassing and it's all Arthur's fault. And we still have no idea where Henry is.

mystery bed

8:00PM
MY BEDROOM, IN A MOOD WITH ARTHUR

I just hope Watson is still wearing that moustache when he comes back. It's the best in our collection. It's Arthur's fault that Watson ran off wearing it, so he WILL be replacing it with his pocket money if it's lost.

LOST

At least there's some other cool stuff to look forward to. It's Puddleford Festival time again! Poppy says we have to synchronise our alarm clocks on Saturday because you need to arrive early if you don't want to queue for the totally spooky ghost train or the helter-skelter.

Helter-Skelter

violet

GHOST TRAIN

Poppy

me

Oh, and I've discovered that this year's festival theme, Pioneers of Puddleford, is actually nothing to do with pies. Pioneers of Puddleford are actually people who have achieved great things and made Puddleford a cool place to live.

LADY WINKLETON: Set up Puddleford Museum one hundred years ago. We totally solved a mystery about her stuffed poodle.

LIZBETH FELANGE: Founded Kitty Yum Luxury Cat Products, here in Puddleford. Kitty Yum is now a massive worldwide success and this year's festival sponsor.

MUM (AKA MRS MYSTERY): Runs online knitting shop called Knitted Fancies (You Name It, We'll Knit It). The first person ever to knit a miniature model of Puddleford. She's running a Knit Your Own Miniature Puddleford demonstration at the festival.

miniature PUDDLEFORD

me → inventing stuff

I couldn't believe it when our totally ace class teacher, Miss Crumble, announced that we'd all be entering a new Best in Show Young Inventors competition at the festival. Everyone in our school is going to get a chance to be a Pioneer of Puddleford too! We are even going to have another Pioneer of Puddleford helping us all week in school – a real-life inventor!

HORATIO TWEED: We met Horatio briefly once while doing a surveillance sweep of Puddleford. (The Young Super Sleuth's Handbook recommends this if things are a bit quiet.) He looks like a proper mad scientist but his house on Blossom Lane is totally normal. I bet he has to make it seem that way so nobody suspects he's making amazing top-secret inventions inside.

Horatio Tweed

Detectives in films always have a genius inventor friend with a mysterious nickname, like Z or Nuts, who makes gadgets for them – like lunchboxes that turn into rocket packs.* We could be sitting in the school dinner hall, and if a call came in about an urgent mystery situation – WHOOSH! – we'd fire up the lunchbox and jet off to investigate before the teachers could say anything.

Maybe Horatio will agree to be our cool inventor friend who will do stuff like that for us? I hope so!

LUNCH

WOW!

LUNCH

looks normal

*THE LUNCH LAUNCHER was one of the brilliant ideas that me, Poppy and Violet came up with as part of our homework. Miss Crumble said we can work together. Yay!

Deduction 'o' matic

BOBBLE HAT CAM

Monday 20th April

Extending sticky fingers CRIMINAL CATCHER!

cunning case
(pencil case walkie-talkie)

GADGETS AND MYSTERY SOLVING

Sometimes fake moustaches and dark sunglasses are not enough. Gadgets will make you the most envied detective in town but it's essential to pick the right device for the type of mystery situation you are in.

Types of Gadget:

Basic walkie-talkie

High-tech walkie-talkie

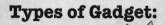

Communication

Homemade walkie-talkie

Surveillance

Comfort surveillance inflatable chair

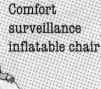

Lunchbox binoculars

Concealed camera devices

Suspect Capturing

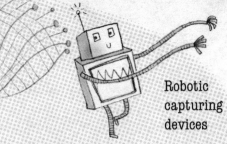

Net launchers

Robotic capturing devices

Battery powered skates (for chase situations)

Fancy gadgets

X-ray specs

Cough-it-up confession sweets

I dunnit!

Rocket-powered underpants

WARNING

Don't let Fancy Gadget Fever cloud your mystery senses. We hear many stories of detective teams falling apart after heated arguments over whose turn it is to use the new gadget or about whose gadget is the best.